Chuck is a Quest
and
Pat is Fed Up

Level 3 – Yellow

Helpful Hints for Reading at Home

The graphemes (written letters) and phonemes (units of sound) used throughout this series are aligned with Letters and Sounds. This offers a consistent approach to learning whether reading at home or in the classroom. Books levelled as 'a' are an introduction to this band. Readers can advance to 'b' where graphemes are consolidated and further graphemes are introduced.

HERE IS A LIST OF ALTERNATIVE GRAPHEMES FOR THIS PHASE OF LEARNING. AN EXAMPLE OF THE PRONUNCIATION CAN BE FOUND IN BRACKETS.

Phase 3			
j (jug)	v (van)	w (wet)	x (fox)
y (yellow)	z (zoo)	zz (buzz)	qu (quick)
ch (chip)	sh (shop)	th (thin/then)	ng (ring)
ai (rain)	ee (feet)	igh (night)	oa (boat)
oo (boot/look)	ar (farm)	or (for)	ur (hurt)
ow (cow)	oi (coin)	ear (dear)	air (fair)
ure (sure)	er (corner)		

HERE ARE SOME WORDS WHICH YOUR CHILD MAY FIND TRICKY.

Phase 3 Tricky Words			
he	you	she	they
we	all	me	are
be	my	was	her

HERE ARE SOME WORDS THAT MIGHT NOT YET BE FULLY DECODABLE.

Challenge Words			
quest	pond	chimps	splash

TOP TIPS FOR HELPING YOUR CHILD TO READ:

- Allow children time to break down unfamiliar words into units of sound and then encourage children to string these sounds together to create the word.

- Encourage your child to point out any focus phonics when they are used.

- Read through the book more than once to grow confidence.

- Ask simple questions about the text to assess understanding.

- Encourage children to use illustrations as prompts.

PHASE 3
3a

This book is an 'a' level and is a yellow level 3 book band.

Chuck is on a Quest
and
Pat is Fed Up

Written by
Robin Twiddy

Illustrated by
Amy Li

Can you say this sound and draw it with your finger?

Chuck is on a Quest

Written by
Robin Twiddy

Illustrated by
Amy Li

Chuck is on a quest. Chuck needs to go to the den.

Look! The pond of pongs and shells.

Chuck is on the hill of the chill chimps.

It is a big quest. Chuck will not quit.

Up the hill of big chins. Chuck cannot quit.

Shush, Chuck! This is the hall of naps.

Chuck is on a quest, but he will not quit.

Chuck is on a path. Look at the men.

It is the den. Chuck needs to hit the duck to get in.

The den is full of cash.

Be quick, Chuck. Get all of the cash.

It is the end of the quest. Chuck needs to go back. It will not be quick!

Can you match the object to the sound that it starts with?

ch qu sh

Pat is Fed Up

Written by
Robin Twiddy

Illustrated by
Amy Li

Pat is a chicken and Pat is fed up.

Can Pat be a duck and go up, up and up?

Quack, quack, crash. Pat cannot go up, up and up.

Pat is a chicken and Pat is fed up.

Can Pat be a fish and splash, splash, splash?

Pat cannot splash, splash, splash!
Pat is wet!

Pat is a chicken and she is fed up.

Can Pat be a cat and rush quick, quick, quick?

But Pat cannot rush. Pat is not quick. Puff, puff, puff!

Pat is a chicken and she is fed up.

Until she feels it happen. An egg!

Pat is a chicken and that is good.

©2020 **BookLife Publishing Ltd.**
King's Lynn, Norfolk PE30 4LS

ISBN 978-1-83927-282-0

All rights reserved. Printed in Malaysia.
A catalogue record for this book is available from
the British Library.

Chuck is on a Quest & Pat is Fed Up
Written by Robin Twiddy
Illustrated by Amy Li

An Introduction to BookLife Readers...

Our Readers have been specifically created in line with the London Institute of Education's approach to book banding and are phonetically decodable and ordered to support each phase of the Letters and Sounds document.

Each book has been created to provide the best possible reading and learning experience. Our aim is to share our love of books with children, providing both emerging readers and prolific page-turners with beautiful books that are guaranteed to provoke interest and learning, regardless of ability.

BOOK BAND GRADED using the Institute of Education's approach to levelling.

PHONETICALLY DECODABLE supporting each phase of Letters and Sounds.

EXERCISES AND QUESTIONS to offer reinforcement and to ascertain comprehension.

BEAUTIFULLY ILLUSTRATED to inspire and provoke engagement, providing a variety of styles for the reader to enjoy whilst reading through the series.

AUTHOR INSIGHT:
ROBIN TWIDDY

Robin Twiddy is one of BookLife Publishing's most creative and prolific editorial talents, who imbues all his copy with a sense of adventure and energy. Robin's Cambridge-based first class honours degree in psychosocial studies offers a unique viewpoint on factual information and allows him to relay information in a manner that readers of any age are guaranteed to retain. He also has a certificate in Teaching in the Lifelong Sector, and a post graduate certificate in Consumer Psychology. A father of two, Robin has written over 70 titles for BookLife and specialises in conceptual, role-playing narratives which promote interaction with the reader and inspire even the most reluctant of readers to fully engage with his books.

This book is an 'a' level and is a yellow level 3 book band.

Additional images courtesy of Shutterstock.com.
Chuck is on a Quest p6-7 – Alfmaler, p8-9 Kriengsuk Prasroetsung, p14-15 – peiyang, HappyPictures, p16-17 – peiyang, HappyPictures
Pat is Fed Up p20-21 – Kriengsuk Prasroetsung, Jiffy Avril, p22-23 – Kriengsuk Prasroetsung, p24-25 – Kriengsuk Prasroetsung, Jiffy Avril, p26-27 – Kriengsuk Prasroetsung, Jiffy Avril, p28-29 – Kriengsuk Prasroetsung, p30-31 – Kriengsuk Prasroetsung, Peshkova, AVN Photo Lab